IT C............................VORSE

IT COULD ALWAYS BE WORSE

A Yiddish folk tale retold and with pictures by

MARGOT ZEMACH

SCHOLASTIC INC.

New York   Toronto   London   Auckland   Sydney

ISBN 0-590-41661-8

Copyright © 1976 by Margot Zemach. All rights reserved. Published by
Scholastic Inc., 730 Broadway, New York, NY 10003, by
arrangement with Farrar, Straus & Giroux, Inc.

12 11 10 9 8 7 6 5 4 3 2 1   7 8 9/8 0 1/9

Printed in the U.S.A.   08

To my friend Gina, with love

Once upon a time in a small village a poor unfortunate man lived with his mother, his wife, and his six children in a little one-room hut. Because they were so crowded, the man and his wife often argued. The children were noisy, and they fought. In winter, when the nights were long and the days were cold, life was especially hard. The hut was full of crying and quarreling. One day, when the poor unfortunate man couldn't stand it any more, he ran to the Rabbi for advice.

"Holy Rabbi," he cried, "things are in a bad way with me, and getting worse. We are so poor that my mother, my wife, my six children, and I all live together in one small hut. We are too crowded, and there's so much noise. Help me, Rabbi. I'll do whatever you say."

The Rabbi thought and pulled on his beard. At last he said, "Tell me, my poor man, do you have any animals, perhaps a chicken or two?"

"Yes," said the man. "I do have a few chickens, also a rooster and a goose."

"Ah, fine," said the Rabbi. "Now go home and take the chickens, the rooster, and the goose into your hut to live with you."

"Yes indeed, Rabbi," said the man, though he was a bit surprised.

The poor unfortunate man hurried home and took the chickens, the rooster, and the goose out of the shed and into his little hut.

When some days or a week had gone by, life in the hut was worse than before. Now with the quarreling and crying there was honking, crowing, and clucking. There were feathers in the soup. The hut stayed just as small and the children grew bigger. When the poor unfortunate man couldn't stand it any longer, he again ran to the Rabbi for help.

"Holy Rabbi," he cried, "see what a misfortune has befallen me. Now with the crying and quarreling, with the honking, clucking, and crowing, there are feathers in the soup. Rabbi, it couldn't be worse. Help me, please."

The Rabbi listened and thought. At last he said, "Tell me, do you happen to have a goat?"

"Oh, yes, I do have an old goat, but he's not worth much."

"Excellent," said the Rabbi. "Now go home and take the old goat into your hut to live with you."

"Ah, no! Do you really mean it, Rabbi?" cried the man.

"Come, come now, my good man, and do as I say at once," said the Rabbi.

The poor unfortunate man tramped back home with his head hanging down and took the old goat into his hut.

When some days or a week had gone by, life in the little hut was much worse. Now, with the crying, quarreling, clucking, honking, and crowing, the goat went wild, pushing and butting everyone with his horns. The hut seemed smaller, the children grew bigger.

When the poor unfortunate man couldn't stand it another minute, he again ran to the Rabbi.

"Holy Rabbi, help me!" he screamed. "Now the goat is running wild. My life is a nightmare."

The Rabbi listened and thought. At last he said, "Tell me, my poor man. Is it possible that you have a cow? Young or old doesn't matter."

"Yes, Rabbi, it's true I have a cow," said the poor man fearfully.

"Go home then," said the Rabbi, "and take the cow into your hut."

"Oh, no, surely not, Rabbi!" cried the man.

"Do it at once," said the Rabbi.

The poor unfortunate man trudged home with a heavy heart and took the cow into his hut. Is the Rabbi crazy? he thought.

When some days or a week had gone by, life in the hut was very much worse than before. Everyone quarreled, even the chickens. The goat ran wild. The cow trampled everything. The poor man could hardly believe his misfortune. At last, when he could stand it no longer, he ran to the Rabbi for help.

"Holy Rabbi," he shrieked, "help me, save me, the end of the world has come! The cow is trampling everything. There is no room even to breathe. It's worse than a nightmare!"

The Rabbi listened and thought. At last he said, "Go home now, my poor unfortunate man, and let the animals out of your hut."

"I will, I will, I'll do it right away," said the man.

The poor unfortunate man hurried home and let the cow, the goat, the chickens, the goose, and the rooster out of his little hut.

That night the poor man and all his family slept peacefully. There was no crowing, no clucking, no honking. There was plenty of room to breathe.

The very next day the poor man ran back to the Rabbi.

"Holy Rabbi," he cried, "you have made life sweet for me. With just my family in the hut, it's so quiet, so roomy, so peaceful . . . What a pleasure!"